MAKING FRIENDS WITH MY EMOTIONS

IT'S OK TO BE ANGRY

THERESA EMMINIZER

PowerKiDS press

Published in 2025 by The Rosen Publishing Group, Inc.
2544 Clinton Street, Buffalo, NY 14224

First Edition

Editor: Theresa Emminizer
Book Design: Michael Flynn

Photo Credits: Cover, pp. 1, 9 Krakenimages.com/Shutterstock.com; (series background) Sergei Mishchenko/Shutterstock.com; p. 5 PR Image Factory/Shutterstock.com; p. 7 StockImageFactory.com/Shutterstock.com; p. 11 H_Ko/Shutterstock.com; p. 13 Kat Om/Shutterstock.com; p. 15 Slatan/Shutterstock.com; p. 17 Ground Picture/Shutterstock.com; p. 19 fizkes/Shutterstock.com; p. 21 Roman Choknadii/Shutterstock.com.

Library of Congress Cataloging-in-Publication Data

Names: Emminizer, Theresa, author.
Title: It's ok to be angry / Theresa Emminizer.
Description: [Buffalo] : PowerKids Press, [2025] | Series: Making friends with my emotions | Includes bibliographical references and index. |
Audience: Grades K-1
Identifiers: LCCN 2023054210 (print) | LCCN 2023054211 (ebook) | ISBN 9781499444964 (library binding) | ISBN 9781499444957 (paperback) | ISBN 9781499444971 (ebook)
Subjects: LCSH: Anger in children–Juvenile literature. | Anger–Juvenile literature.
Classification: LCC BF723.A4 E46 2025 (print) | LCC BF723.A4 (ebook) |
DDC 155.4/1247–dc23/eng/20231218
LC record available at https://lccn.loc.gov/2023054210
LC ebook record available at https://lccn.loc.gov/2023054211

Manufactured in the United States of America

CONTENTS

Anger in Your Body

When you're angry, it might feel like heat rushing through your body. Your stomach might feel tight. You might want to yell. That's OK! Anger is a natural part of life. It's an emotion, or feeling, that everyone feels. You can even make friends with your anger!

Why Do We Feel Angry?

Anger doesn't feel good. But just like all other feelings, it's important. Sometimes anger is trying to tell us something. We may feel angry because we're tired or **hungry**. Or because we're sad or afraid. We may feel angry because something is unfair or because we're unsafe.

Angry or Afraid?

Jayden's mom worked late, so Jayden had to spend every afternoon at his neighbor Mr. Bailey's house. Jayden didn't like it there. It smelled bad and Mr. Bailey was always watching loud, scary movies. Jayden felt alone, helpless, and afraid. That made him angry!

Tell Somebody

It's important to let your feelings out. Pushing down or **ignoring** your anger can even make you sick. Talk to a grown-up you trust. A safe adult will never shame you, or make you feel bad, about your anger. They'll listen and help you.

Scary Inside

Lily was scared of her anger. It felt like a monster inside her. It made her want to yell and throw things. Sometimes, she even wanted to hurt somebody. When Lily was angry, she felt out of control. She didn't know what to do!

Coping with Anger

You don't need to be afraid of your anger. You don't need to let it take over either! Here are some ways to **cope** with anger in a healthy way:

- Do jumping jacks
- Run as fast as you can
- Sing a loud song

Let It Out!

When Danny got mad, it helped to move. He liked to run or ride his bike. But sometimes, he was stuck indoors. When that happened, Danny wrote in his **journal**. Writing about his feelings seemed to move the mad out of his body.

You're Not Alone

Feeling angry doesn't mean you're a bad person. Everyone feels angry sometimes. It's a natural and healthy part of being a person. You don't need to feel **ashamed** of anger or pretend it's not there. It's what you do with your feelings that counts.

Making Friends with Anger

Remember, feelings come, and feelings go. When you're angry, it helps to know that you won't feel that way forever. Next time you find yourself feeling angry, notice what's happening in your body. Take a deep breath. It's OK to be angry.

GLOSSARY

ashamed: Feeling shame, or feeling bad due to something you may have done.

cope: Dealing with or working through your feelings.

hungry: Feeling uneasy or in pain due to the need to eat.

ignore: To pretend something isn't happening.

journal: A blank book used to write down personal thoughts and feelings; a diary.

FOR MORE INFORMATION

BOOKS

McAneney, Caitie. *I Talk to Cope.* New York, NY: PowerKids Press, 2023.

Wood, John. *Anita the Alligator Feels Angry.* New York, NY: Rosen Publishing, 2020.

WEBSITES

Kids Health
kidshealth.org/en/kids/anger.html
Learn more about anger and healthy ways to cope with it.

PBS Kids
pbskids.org/learn/lifes-little-lessons/mad-feelings/
Find more ways to calm down when you feel mad.

INDEX